30
D0260050

...e returned on or befo.e
... nped belo v.

Elephant Hide and Seek

A humorous
story

First published in 2006 by
Franklin Watts
338 Euston Road
London
NW1 3BH

Franklin Watts Australia
Hachette Children's Books
Level 17/207 Kent Street
Sydney
NSW 2000

Text © Rosemary Billam 2006
Illustration © Ali Lodge 2006

The rights of Rosemary Billam to be identified as the
author and Ali Lodge as the illustrator of this Work
have been asserted in accordance with the Copyright,
Designs and Patents Act, 1988.

All rights reserved. No part of this publication may be
reproduced, stored in a retrieval system, or transmitted
in any form or by any means, electronic, mechanical,
photocopy, recording or otherwise, without the prior
written permission of the copyright owner.

A CIP catalogue record for this book is available
from the British Library.

ISBN 0 7496 6549 1 (hbk)
ISBN 0 7496 6556 4 (pbk)

Series Editor: Jackie Hamley
Series Advisors: Dr Barrie Wade, Dr Hilary Minns
Design: Peter Scoulding

Printed in China

LONDON BOROUGH OF SUTTON LIBRARY SERVICE	
02430500 7	
Askews	Nov-2006
JF	

Elephant
Hide and Seek

Written by
Rosemary Billam

Illustrated by
Ali Lodge

W
FRANKLIN WATTS
LONDON•SYDNEY

Rosemary Billam

"I love playing hide and seek. I'm sure elephants have just as much fun playing the game. And they have a lot more to hide!"

Ali Lodge

"I loved playing hide and seek when I was younger with my brother and sister, just like Flo and Baby. My favourite hiding place was behind the curtains! Where is yours?"

One morning, Mother Elephant
decided to have a swim.

"Keep an eye on Baby
for me, Flo!" she said.
"Yes, Mother," said Flo.

But when Flo looked around,

Baby was nowhere to be seen.

Flo soon found Baby playing
with some young rhinos.
"I thought you'd got lost!" said Flo.

"How did you find me?" asked Baby. "It was easy. You're the only one with a trunk!" said Flo.

"Let's play hide and seek," said Baby.

Flo wondered if this was a good idea.

But still she covered her eyes and counted to ten. "I'm coming!" she called.

"That's a funny-looking
tree," thought Flo.
"Got you!" she cried.

"How did you find me?" asked Baby.

"Trees don't usually have ears!"

said Flo.

The sun was high in the sky.

"Can I have another go?"

asked Baby. "All right," agreed Flo.

Baby ran away as fast as he could.

"Coming, ready or not!" Flo called.

Flo soon heard a strange panting noise coming from a cave. Baby was still out of breath after his run.

"Got you!" cried Flo.

"How did you find me?" asked Baby.

"I followed my ears!" said Flo.

"Can I have another go?"
asked Baby.

"All right," his sister agreed.
"But don't go too far. Mother will
wonder where we are."

Baby covered himself with leaves.
But he left one of his back legs
sticking out and Flo tripped over it.

"Got you!" cried Flo.

"Can I have one last go?"
asked Baby.

This time it was too easy. Baby's tail
was sticking out of a bush.
"He never learns!" thought Flo,
as she pounced on his tail.

But the tail belonged to a wart-hog and he was not pleased. He looked so fierce that Flo turned and fled.

Flo ran as fast as she could to the lake and hid in the water. The sun was beginning to set.

"I'll never find Baby now," Flo sobbed.
Then she felt something pull her tail.
"Help!" she thought. "The wart-hog
must have followed me."

"Got you!" shouted Baby.

"Where did you come from?"
asked Flo in surprise.

"I was hiding in the mud
where you couldn't see me."

"Very clever," said his sister.

"I won that time," said Baby.

"Yes," agreed Flo. "I think you
did. Now let's find Mother!"

Notes for parents and teachers

READING CORNER has been structured to provide maximum support for new readers. The stories may be used by adults for sharing with young children. Primarily, however, the stories are designed for newly independent readers, whether they are reading these books in bed at night, or in the reading corner at school or in the library.

Starting to read alone can be a daunting prospect. READING CORNER helps by providing visual support and repeating words and phrases, while making reading enjoyable. These books will develop confidence in the new reader, and encourage a love of reading that will last a lifetime!

If you are reading this book with a child, here are a few tips:

1. Make reading fun! Choose a time to read when you and the child are relaxed and have time to share the story.

2. Encourage children to reread the story, and to retell the story in their own words, using the illustrations to remind them what has happened.

3. Give praise! Remember that small mistakes need not always be corrected.

READING CORNER covers three grades of early reading ability, with three levels at each grade. Each level has a certain number of words per story, indicated by the number of bars on the spine of the book, to allow you to choose the right book for a young reader:

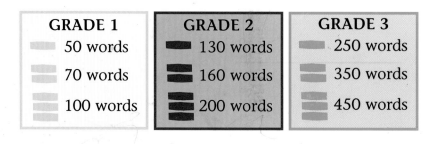

GRADE 1	GRADE 2	GRADE 3
50 words	130 words	250 words
70 words	160 words	350 words
100 words	200 words	450 words